I0538422

CASSIDY'S
ladder

Cassidy's Ladder, 2017,
Joseph Picard

Preface note: While this story follows the events of the novel *Watching Yute*, having read it is not at all necessary to fully understand Cassidy's Ladder. Similarly, while *Watching Yute* involves science-fiction aspects, *Cassidy's Ladder* does not.

While writing Watching Yute, I knew it would end in a less than cheery place. I knew wrapping it up with a happy ending would remove much of the meaning of the book, which resulted in leaving Cassidy in a deep state of mourning.

During the writing, I realized I'd given a doomed character the same first name as a friend who killed herself ten years prior. This ended up influencing the entire book. I kept the same name for the character. Renaming her for my comfort felt disingenuous.

The survivor, Cassidy, was doomed to suffer loss as I did. It's been about eighteen years since my friend Cheryl died. It's been about five years since Watching Yute was published, and the character Cheryl died. Cassidy has been in mourning since then. I always knew I'd be writing about Cassidy again; that I'd need to give her more than a little cameo. She needed help up. This is her time.

For information, feedback or other questions, contact the author.

Joseph Picard joe@ozero.ca

Cover art by Joseph Picard
Other books by Joseph can be found at www.ozero.ca

/// WARNING! \\\

This book is written using a form of English which is somewhat more *English* than *some* readers in *some* regions may be accustomed to.

As such, be advised that colour will be spelled with a 'u', as will honour, valour, neighbour, and so on.

However, I've come to realize that I don't write in UK English. It's Canadian English, so... good bloody luck, reader!

Day 1

Cassidy Stanton's remote desert post had long ago become home, but it never quite regained its natural majesty since the day her fiance was murdered in the line of duty. Justice was had, but it couldn't bring Cheryl back.

She hadn't moved on. She didn't see a reason to. Not to say she was cold to others, but when the quiet came to Cassidy, it came screaming. Over five years, she'd been able to push it back. A little more at a time, but it was there. It used to try to kill her, but now, it only told her she was better off alone.

Here at the base where Cheryl died, there were still friends. Friends that Cassidy counted as family.

"You're going to Brandy's?" asked Maxine, Cassidy's sister-in-arms.

"Yeah. I have all sorts of free time backed up still," Cassidy replied, with a glance toward the helipad.

"This is becoming a habit." Maxine smirked. "Is this a *thing*? They say you shouldn't go back to your exes."

Brandy was a civilian, but also a person Cassidy could talk to in a different way. Brandy represented the civilian world. Something far from the world Cheryl had died in."It's not like that. She's a friend. The les community, such as it is, ain't exactly vast, and I certainty haven't been part of that scene, being out here on base."

Maxine smirked lewdly, and nodded. "Now you're getting into a lesbian *scene*? Damn, girl! Greek bath house hangouts?"

"Shut it. I have my army brothers and sisters here, and I have my... sisterhood sisters. Even if my corner of it is pretty darn small. It's... community. Camaraderie. Some bridges won't burn."

Maxine punched Cassidy softly in the arm. "You know we're all here for you."

Looking to the distant other end of the compound, to the area where her fiance was killed, Cassidy adjusted her cap and gave Maxine a quick hug... And vengeful little punch in the arm. "Yeah. I know. It's sometimes hard to relax around here, not that I could ever transfer out."

"See ya in a week, Cass. Have fun," Maxine ordered.

Cassidy only gave a single nod to answer, and headed to catch her ride.

The Densfarn airport was as busy as ever. In the greater flow of people coming out of the gates, the main area had much more vertical space than need be, and a glass ceiling, presumably to impress investors and tourists alike. Then again, a four-metre high drywall ceiling would make the vast mass of people seem all the more cramped.

Not needing to check her bag in, having come via military transport, Cassidy immediately began scanning the flow of people for Brandy's wavy dark mane. It wasn't needed, as Cassidy's sand-cammo uniform made it easier for Brandy to spot Cassidy first.

"*Hey, desert rat!*"

Cassidy spun to face the call, and her dirty-blonde ponytail swung from the clasp opening in the back of her cap.

"Brandy! Hey! Have you been waiting long?"

They shared a hug, as old friends tend to do. "Naw, Cass, like ten minutes. What do you say we pop by my place, you can dump your stuff, maybe change into something less 'grr', then we can go grab something to eat? After traffic and crap, it'll basically be time for dinner."

Brandy was dressed pretty casually, but Brandy's *public casual* was fairly professional. Dark slacks, flats, navy-blue crossover blouse, and thin silver jewellery dangling loosely from her neck and a wrist.

"Oh, one thing..." Brandy leaned in to Cassidy. For a moment, Cassidy thought she was about to be kissed, and her eyes found themselves fixating on Brandy's and a bit down her neckline.

Before she realized what was happening, Brandy grabbed her hat by the brim, and expertly pulled it up, back, and down off Cassidy's ponytail. The ponytail was still held in tact by a regular hair band. Brandy put the hat on herself, and grinned mischievously.

"No hat for you. No grumpy Cass mode," Brandy said, pulling the brim low over her eyes, "though I won't ask you to let your hair out of the ponytail." They both knew what that would mean, and *that* hadn't happened between them for the better part of a decade.

"I don't know, Brandy. If the wrong people see me without my hat, the whole nation could be in peril."

"I'll chance it."

Getting into the car, Brandy noticed Cassidy adjusting a leather strap around her neck.

"You're still wearing that?" Brandy asked, softly.

Cassidy loosened her jacket and looked down her top at the pendant. A little metal cylinder.

"Yes. It...it's her. You know that."

In a less jovial mood, Brandy took the car out of park, and got them underway. "It's morbid, Cass. Still wearing the engagement ring, I get, I guess, but the little container of ashes..." Brandy sighed, and glanced over to Cassidy. Cassidy was staring dead-eyed forward.

"I'm sorry," Brandy said, giving Cassidy's knee a pat. "I'll shut up about it."

Brandy's townhouse was welcoming, and tidy in a way that one tidies up when expecting company. The evidence of regular, sloppy life lay just under the surface. A front closet that looked tidy until you opened it, a full dishwasher that Brandy probably ran just before going to the airport, that sort of thing. Cassidy had been here before, but Brandy *had* moved since their breakup about seven years ago, so it didn't overtly dig up any memories of their time together.

"I'm taking the damned couch this time!" Cassidy said, tossing her bag next to it.

"Nope! Momma raised me right. Guests get the bed, I'm on the couch, no questioning it."

4

That was a little like how their relationship started. A little too tipsy after dinner with a group of friends, walking to her old place... getting talking, getting the bed, while Brandy took the couch. And later, not so much couch. Fond memories, but it was the past.

"So... fuck cooking? We're going to Guido's for dinner," Brandy decreed.

"Not ordering in?"

"Nah. I have you for a week, and we're not going to spend the week bent over a cardboard box of pizza."

"I like pizza." Cassidy shrugged.

"You like Guido's pizza better." Brandy guided Cassidy to the bedroom, carrying her bag for her. She dumped the bag on the bed, then looked at her clothing. "Good enough for Guido. Cass, I'll be in the kitchen, get civilian already. Nice civilian. A skirt won't kill you. I know I'm wearing pants, shut up." And then she left the room and closed the door to give Cassidy privacy.

Cassidy smirked. Getting ordered around made it clearer that Brandy wasn't coming on to her.

"Yes Sir!" Cassidy called to her through the door.

"No Sir-ing! Civilian time! Skirt!"

Fine. She started pulling things out of her bag, and found the only skirt she owned. She didn't wear it much. A simple black thing, stopping just above the knee. She'd had it a long time.

She wore it to Cheryl's funeral. It was hard to believe it had been that long.

Stop it. It's just a skirt. She put it on, and ditched her desert cammo jacket. The white tank top looked civilian enough. The boots did not. If they were polished and glossy, they might pass as chic in a punky sort of way, but no, they were showing their age, and where they'd been quite clearly. She pulled out a pair of black runners. They were sleek enough to pass as a fashion choice, and went with the skirt. She let her hair loose, only long enough to give it a quick brush, and back into the ponytail.

She stepped out to go find Brandy, who didn't hear her coming, since she was making noise putting away dishes. Cassidy took a moment to admire this woman that she once loved so much, yet drove away with neglect. Citing being busy. Duty and so forth. This was true, mostly. Mostly. But even after all the years, it still felt a bit hollow. Like it was her fault; that she could have easily done more. It was true.

They were little more than girls when they started dating, but time had turned them into women. Wiser maybe, a little. Cassidy realized she was just watching this woman. Her hair was more or less the same as it ever was, her figure... maybe it was different. Not lesser by any stretch of the imagination, but different. Maybe it was in the way she moved. But this was a woman, no girl. The same could likely be said of herself.

This woman would always be part of her life. She blocked Cassidy's calls shortly after the breakup, but when the news of Cheryl's death became known, Brandy was there with concern. She cared, and even though she couldn't stake claim to any military bond, it seemed obvious that Brandy would always be around as a true friend.

Cassidy only snapped out of watching Brandy when Brandy finished with putting away dishes, and closed the dishwasher.

"Cass, hello? Are you in there?"

Cassidy laughed it off. "Oh, yeah, hi. Kinda spaced out for a moment. Call it a symptom of decompressing from work."

"Or decompression after getting out of those boots. I wouldn't take you to the Oscars in the outfit you have on now, but at least you look like there's a potential to relax."

"Are you making fun of the shoes, the skirt, or the tank top?"

Brandy leaned back, and looked Cassidy up and down. "I can't decide."

"Oh, stuff it. Like you said, we're not going to the Oscars, we're going to Guido's. Is this under-dressed for Guido's?"

"Borderline. The tank top especially screams *I put no effort into my outfit.*"

"That's because I didn't."

"It shows."

"Get bent."

"Let's go."

Guido's was a vaguely Italian, slightly fashionable place trying to put on an air of 'night club'. A little bit on the intimate side. Background music trying to walk the '*smooth adult contemporary... but hip*' line was playing not-so-softly near the doors. Oak, chrome, and occasional under-lighting did what they did, short of whipping out blacklights.

Guido's wasn't likely chosen for romantic reasons. Cassidy knew that Brandy always liked the place in general.

Cassidy checked out a menu while Brandy talked to the maître d'. Brandy and Cassidy were led to a booth.

A booth with someone already in it.

"Cass, this is Nia," Brandy said, gesturing to the smiling woman. Nia had deliciously entrancing hair, as straight as if she'd just stepped out of a shower. Deep chestnut, with a hint of red highlight. Her eyes were of a similar deep earthiness, and sparkled with her smile.

"Uh, hi Nia. I'm Cassidy, but I suspect you already knew that."

"Guilty!" she answered. "Good to meet you."

As Brandy had just sat opposite of Nia, and wasn't making room for Cassidy, Nia slide over to provide a space.

This was all a trap of some kind. A set up. Cassidy gave Brandy a quick little accusing glance as she sat.

Cassidy thought, "*If Brandy is trying to set me up with Nia... She knows I'm not looking. She knows I'm not ready. This Nia girl is attractive enough and all, but...*" Cassidy clutched her pendant carrying the ashes. Brandy noticed, and her smile faulted for a moment.

The ball fell into Cassidy's court. "So, uh... Nia, I'm in army-guy-business, I guess you know. What do *you* do with your days?"

"I manage a few warehouses down at the docks," Nia said, "and now and then we handle a bit of the smaller pleasure-craft. Not our specialty though."

Cassidy raised an eyebrow. "Gotta say, you clean up pretty well for a dock-hand!"

Nia gave a small chuckle. "I try. To be fair, I just tell dock-hands what to do. Fewer callouses that way."

It was then that the waitress came along to take orders for drinks. Nia went for a margarita, Cassidy for a rum & coke, Brandy ordered a rum & coke – double.

Nia mused at Brandy's stronger order. "Taking an early lead out of the gate, it's Brandy, in the spirits of her name!"

"Oh hush. At least I didn't order a bulldog," Brandy said.

"Dog?"

Cassidy explained to Nia. "A.K.A. the Mexican Bulldog. Take a margarita, then stick an open bottle of corona in, upside down so they mix as you drink."

"Hardrcore," Nia purred, raising an eyebrow to Cassidy. "Maybe later."

When the drinks came, Brandy got suddenly busy with receiving a text. She made an irritated face, and sent a quick reply. "Guys. Dammit, I have to go. I'm not sure how long this is going to take."

"...what...?" Cassidy said flatly.

"Work thing," Brandy explained, "A blueprint needs a revision sent to a foreman by nine tonight, and I was so sure this change wouldn't get accepted, I didn't prep a file with it in there. Man, assumptions, huh? I'm so sorry." She slid her rum and coke *double* across the table over to Cassidy. "That's your fav, have it. You can make it up to me tomorrow."

"Make it up to *you*." Cassidy replied with a sullen glare. The ruse seemed obvious. A moment later, Cassidy was alone with Nia, and three ounces of alcohol with her name on them.

"I guess I can move over to the other side now," Cassidy quipped, slipping around before Nia could have a say in it.

"Ah," Nia said with a sly smile, "Now I get to stare directly at you." And stare she did, doing her best to grope Cassidy with bedroom eyes. At least this new position would prevent a hand from appearing on her knee.

Then Cassidy took a sip of her drink. Maybe a touch of alcohol wouldn't be the worst idea ever. She was starting to feel nearly combative, and that much wasn't necessary. Her commanding officer had tried to get her into meditation in the past, but that never stuck. Deep breath.

Just then, Cassidy felt Nia's nylon-clad foot touch her bare ankle, under the table. Cassidy snapped to lock eyes with the beauty across from her.

"Well. Aren't *you* aggressive?"

Nia closed her eyes and smiled softly. "You're a soldier, I thought you'd be used to that."

Cassidy pulled her ankle away. "My post is exclusively defencive. It's a guard post."

"I know. I'm sure you can handle it, then. Meet any oncoming comings on to, and the like..."

Cassidy looked away. If Nia knew about Cassidy's day failing her duty, she hopefully would have chosen better wording. Unconsciously, she tapped her engagement ring on the edge of the table.

"Ah," Nia murmured, "Brandy told me a bit about that. Is... is that going to be... a problem?"

Cassidy dragged the ring along the edge to meet her other hand. "I wasn't expecting a setup today."

Nia looked down into her drink, a little deflated. She took a long sip through the straw. "You're.. not into the subtleties. The dance, the game. I get that. Honestly, I should have expected it. I guess I'll make it clean cut."

"What do you mean?"

"I mean I'll put my cards on the table, Cass. I'm after something physical. It that turns in something else, great."

Cassidy looked away, and took a deep breath. "Well. Your honesty is refreshing. Admirable, even."

Nia tilted he head, trying to make eye contact, her hair leaning off the side like a dark waterfall. "Well? That doesn't sound good."

"Well. A decade ago. The 'me' I was then would have probably been very interested. Heck, you certainly… clean up *very* nice for a dock hand."

"I kind doubt you would have looked this amazing a decade ago," Nia said, "You *exude* strength, Cass. It's more than a little intimidating, but I want to wrap myself around that strength, and –"

"Look, I don't think I'm your type… you're… pretty. I mean, you obviously work at it. And that's fine. A real legit lipstick lesbian, if you want the cliché label."

"What I want…?" Nia pondered, "do you assume I necessarily want someone like myself?" She flipped a bit of her precisely cut, straight hair for effect.

"I'd pay to watch that," Cassidy mumbled. "Maybe you don't want a girl like yourself… but you don't want someone like me."

"What makes you say that? Your your tough-girl bit is hot."

How was Cassidy going to explain? That she was damaged, that she wasn't into the fast and slick romantic hijinks. That she felt a tiny bit violated being set up and dumped in Nia's lap.

Besides. Nia was superficial. Pretty. Too pretty.

Cassidy slammed back the rest of her drink, and set the glass down a tiny bit harder than she intended. "Look, Nia, I'm sorry this isn't going how you were expecting." She pushed Brandy's drink away from both of them. "But I'm just not in the market." She tapped her ring on the table twice. "So yeah. I guess it *is* this that's the problem." She got up, preparing to leave.

Nia looked up to Cassidy, in a softer, less practice voice than she's been using so far. "How… how long are you going to let that be a problem?"

"As long as she remains dead," Cassidy growled. Nia looked away and took a deep breath. "I don't mean to be a bitch," Cassidy said, "Just forget about me, keep it simple. Sorry."

Still staring into the dwindling margarita, Nia meekly stated, "I wasn't asking for my own benefit. How long? It's…"

"Forever I guess. It's not healthy, yeah, I know. I've heard it. That's the way it is."

Cassidy arrived (by taxi, thank you very much) to Brandy's place, and entered after a doorbell ring.

Brandy, wearing a look of concern, soon found Cassidy, "So, you and Nia... You didn't get along?"

Cassidy shrugged with a grunt. "Shes not my type. A little too... well, I don't like to slap a label on someone I barely know, but... a bit superficial? A little... overly... overt?"

"Yeah," Brandy tilted her head in mock sympathy. "But that'll happen when someone's coming on to a person."

Cassidy grunted again. "She's too pretty. Too pretty for me."

"Cass, that sounds awful! She had a chance to dress up a little. If I wasn't so concerned with surprising --"

"Ambushing. You mean ambushing."

Brandy sighed. "Cass, I was just hoping..."

Cassidy gave a long sigh to go with a long, tired stare. "You were hoping what. That I'd fuck my way into getting over Cheryl?"

"No! Well possibly. If that happened, it would at least have been something. Honestly, I wouldn't have bet the farm on you and Nia getting together."

"So what was the grand plan, then?"

"I... I don't know. Kick you out of a rut, maybe. Show you there are still fish out there."

"Cheryl can't be just *replaced* like that!"

"No. I know." Brandy sighed, but was not surprised. "I know as well as anyone who knows you at all, that Cheryl will always be part of you." Brandy took Cassidy's hand, and looked into her eyes. "But you have to be a part of the living world, too. This... it's killing you."

Cassidy broke eye contact, looking away before tears asserted themselves. But she squeezed Brandy's hand back. "It certainly has tried to kill me a few times." Her C.O. had taken away her gun, and eventually forced her into counseling. If her post required her to carry a gun, and the unit wasn't such a family, she knows she would be out of the military. Still, that might be wise. If the counselor had been told of the suicide attempt, she'd definitely be in a different position now. It had been a couple of years since she'd seen the counselor.

She was considered fully fit for duty. It never really felt that way. She'd been a bit of a mess before meeting Cheryl. Cassidy had quietly looked down on people who couldn't be reasonably happy unless they were in a relationship, but she had to accept that she was apparently one of them.

She hated that. It made her feel weak. Unworthy. Especially not befitting of a solider.

"Brandy, I'm worn out. A bit of jetlag, too. I think I'm going to hit the hay."

"Is this a *I'm okay, I'm just tired, not depressed* situation?"

"....no."

"Bullshit. I'm making popcorn, you go pick a movie."

While Brandy to went on a quest in cupboards to find a pack of microwave popcorn, Cassidy poked at the TV remote to find movies. Super hero destruction-porn, desperately dull awards attempts, comedies that looked too much like last year's selection, and the year before that.

Oh look, romantic comedies. Page after page of hetero love, between copy/paste actors, likely in copy/paste stories. She didn't bother hunting for lesbian tales, that would be even more awkward with Brandy than the hetero ones. Better to avoid romance altogether.

Oh look, a semi-snobby looking science fiction. She hadn't heard anything *bad* about it, an adventure with aliens or anomalies of the week seemed neutral enough.

Cassidy called out to Brandy, "How about The Ganymede Event?"

"Whatever, sure," Brandy replied as the popcorn beeped. "What's it about?"

"I think it's a bunch of supermodels trying to act like they're smart. And they go to Ganymede."

"And have an event," Brandy added.

"Ahh! No spoilers!"

Brandy sat down next to Cassidy, and handed her the searing hot pack of popcorn. "Yeah, and I heard people participate, or are otherwise affected by said event."

"My lord, how do they come up with these?" Cassidy asked with phony awe.

"Unholy contract with Sagan."

"Oh, of course."

Opening credits began with a little exposition text, then vast distant moon landscapes... this was not going to be a fast-paced flick.

Brandy grabbed a greedy handful of popcorn, then left the rest to Cassidy before making herself comfortable in a lazy slouch in her corner of the sofa. In past times, this would be an invitation to Cassidy to lean against her, and cuddle up for the rest of the movie.

The bloody movie could get moving any time, please. Dialogue? Anything other then establishing shots?

Cassidy opened her mouth hoping something neutral would come out.

"Did you promise to fix Nia up because she'd been going after *you*?" Oops. Not entirely neutral.

Brandy scoffed on a chunk of popcorn. "No!... Maybe. Just a side effect."

"You're awful"

"I'm efficient," Brandy said, trying to sound like it was the most reasonable idea, "if it had all worked out, it would be two birds with one stone! I'm never going to live this down, am I?"

"Nope. What made you think I'd match with her?" Cassidy frowned. "I'm not into those super-pretty types."

Brandy laughed out loud. "*Thanks a ton! Good to know you only dated me cuz I'm an uggo!*"

"No, no, you know what I mean." Cassidy sighed. "You're not like... high maintenance. You're pretty. Just inherently, natural bea–"

"Oh?" Brandy smiled. "*Do go on.*"

Cassidy felt herself blushing. "Just watch the damned movie."

The movie proceeded more or less as expected, doing its best to be 'gripping'. Cassidy found herself only half-watching.

She remained a little peeved about the set-up with Nia. At the same time, part of her wondered if she should have taken the idea less seriously, and just went along with it.

"We could be fucking right *now*." Cassidy mumbled to herself.

"*What?*" Brandy squeaked in surprise..

Cassidy dismissively waved her hand at Brandy. "Not you and me, me and Nia. Hypothetically. If I'd gone with her."

Brandy shook her head and smirked. "Regrets?"

"Tons," Cassidy said as she let her slouch deposit her onto the floor, "but not so much about Nia, if I take half a second to think about it."

"Okay, I'll bite, what's your list of reasons to not go with Nia?"

"Well..." Cassidy toyed with one of the last bits of popcorn. "I've already gone on about the –"

Ringing came from her pocket. Cassidy pulled it out and looked at the screen. "Pete and Sandy." Cheryl's parents. Cassidy tapped to answer, and Sandy's face popped up onscreen.

"Hey Sandy, hows ya?"

"Good, good," the cheerful middle-aged woman answered, "how was the flight?"

"Military. People pay taxes, you'd think they could stock a little bag of peanuts."

"Allergies."

"I didn't join the army to play it safe, ma'am!" Cassidy gave an exaggerated salute.

"Well then, Sergeant,"

"Lieu*tenant*," Cassidy corrected.

"Okay then, Lieutenant, are you brave enough to face my cooking tomorrow night?"

"Salmon?"

"Salmon!"

Cassidy rubbed her jaw sagely. "I've faced this foe before. I think I can handle it."

"This time it will have lemon asparagus as backup."

"Cunning. I'll have to equip myself with some kind of white wine if I plan to be victorious."

"If you like," Sandy said, "but I insist you bring that foot behind you."

Cassidy looked back. On the sofa, Brandy's foot could be seen. Brandy moved around to get her face into the shot. "It's all right, Mrs. Lowe –"

"I thought I said I insist!"

After the call, Brandy and Cassidy continued the movie. The leading couple had their obligatory PG sex scene in slow-motion zero-gravity, then there was some kind of vital crisis which Cassidy didn't fully understand due to barely paying attention to the rest of the movie, he saves her, they save the ship, or base, or whatever, credits.

"So, what did you learn about Ganymede?" Brandy asked.

"It had an incident."

"Bzzzz. Event. It's the Ganymede *Event*."

"Dang. I fail. Now can I go to bed?"

Brandy grimaced. "When were you going to tell me you'd planned dinner at Cheryl's parents' place?"

"Sorry. Is it a big deal? I've gone in past years."

Brandy folded her arms, and stared down into nowhere. "No, it's fine. Doesn't happen to wreck any plans or anything. Not like I own you for the week or anything."

Cassidy patted Brandy's arm. "You'll do fine, they're great people."

Brandy only gave a resigned nod.

Day 2

The next morning, Cassidy woke on the late side, blaming her laziness on jet-lag. The room smelled decidedly like Brandy; a combination of her shampoo and hints of her favourite discrete perfume, which hasn't changed in ages. Falling asleep to it wasn't so bad, either.

Cassidy rolled over, feeling like she might even find Brandy there, and that would have been fine.

Not as if they'd slept together last night, no, no, certainly not.

But it would have been... fine if she were simply *there*.

Unconsciously, in a groggy waking state, she found her hand resting on a nearby pillow, and staring at it.

She felt like calling out to Brandy, to see if she was up, but she dreaded opening her mouth and unleashing morning breath.

She dragged herself out of bed, grabbed her toothbrush and toothpaste before shambling towards the bathroom. She was staring herself down in the bathroom mirror, brushing her teeth, when Brandy's voice passed by.

"Pants?"

Cassidy assessed her situation, and gently kicked the door shut. "Oops."

"Ya run around nekkid from the waist down on base?" Brandy called, now further across the house.

"Only on guard duty, or inspections."

"Thorough inspections! Hey – Bacon and toast?"

"If you're making em, Brandy, I won't say no! So, I'm up early enough for break –"

"It's two PM, dear. But I got bacon because you were coming."

"*You* like bacon," Cassidy said as she slipped back into the bedroom to get dressed quickly.

"Yeah, but I guess not enough to get it just for myself."

Lacking much else to do before having to go to the Sandy and Pete's for dinner, Cassidy and Brandy ended up at a mall; not something Cassidy had a lot of opportunity for, living out in the desert on-base.

An unspoken agreement kept them away from jewellery stores. Cassidy had never been big on the stuff, and it would bring conversation back to her ring, and that morbid little pendant.

"Gonna get stuff for people back at base?" Brandy suggested.

"Well, let's see..." Cassidy looked on into nowhere while she did inventory of her friends. "Frig, they're all kind of hard to buy for. I'd get Cipriana something kinky, but I don't think she'd accept."

"Ah yes, the exquisite, yet painfully straight Cip. You really have a thing for her, huh?"

Cassidy chuckled. "Nothing serious. It's become a running gag. If she and I were on the market, I'd be more worried about her orientation."

"Unless something's happened with Cip, you're both 'on the market', single and whatnot."

"Trying to fix me up again?" Cassidy grumbled.

"Not really." Brandy grabbed Cassidy's hand, and stopped walking, forcing Cassidy to stop as well.

"What? Let's go see if we can find any good pants at –"

Brandy squeezed Cassidy's hand harder, looking at the floor. "Don't be alone."

"What?" Cassidy tried to reclaim her hand, but Brandy had it pretty firmly.

"Don't be alone. It's not good for you."

Cassidy tried to look Brandy in the eye, but Brandy was too busy looking at the floor. She knew that Brandy was talking about her suicide attempts. Cassidy squeezed back. "It wouldn't be healthy to lean on a person like that. It's not fair."

"Not fair to a friend, either. If you die, and I didn't try my best." Brandy's voice cracked at the end.

"Are.. are you cry –"

"Shut up. Follow me."

And follow her, she did. Brandy was practically power-walking, forcing Cassidy to jog a few paces to get by her side. Shortly, they were at a jewellery store. The nearest one was a cheap one, aimed at tweeners. Trash jewellery by some standards, but for the purpose, it was good enough.

"This lady needs a ring, badly," Brandy told the clerk.

The clerk smiled, and took a customer-service stance. "What kind of r –"

"The One ring, or an onion ring, I don't really care, as long as it fits."

"Brandy, what are you doing?" Cassidy wondered out loud.

The clerk brought forward a little rack with simple rings, sorted by size. Playing along a little, Cassidy pointed at the row that was her size.

"Okay," Brandy said brusquely, "pick one."

Cassidy looked to Brandy for any sort of explanation, but Brandy offered none. "Just... pick the that that calls you," Brandy said in a kinder tone.

With a simple blue band of no particular material type chosen, and removed from the rack, Brandy put it onto Cassidy's finger, snug against her engagement ring.

"There," Brandy said with satisfaction.

"What's it mean?" Cassidy asked, "is it to remind me of you or something?"

"No," Brandy began, obviously distressed, "It's... it's to remind you of *you*."

"Brandy, what do you mean, remin–"

"The next time you need to remember her, to remember the dead," Brandy sighed, pushing back the urge to cry, "you'll look at your damned ring, and see the other. It will tell you to remember you. To remember that you're still alive. *Cassidy's alive.*"

Cassidy grabbed Brandy close, fighting tears of her own, trying to escape.

"You're alive," Brandy got out in a wobbly voice against Cassidy's shoulder, "You're still alive."

Going right from the mall, they headed to Sandy and Pete's house. The ride was primarily silent, while Cassidy stared at her new ring. It was a bold colour compared to the engagement ring. She chose it on a whim. Blue is nice, sky is nice, sea is nice. The cheap material seemed unconcerned about the seriousness of its neighbour.

It fell to Brandy to remember that Cassidy implied that they'd be coming with a bottle of white wine. For speed's sake, Brandy ran into the liquor store solo, leaving Cassidy to meditate on her ring.

While they were dating, so long ago, Brandy once bought her a simple bracelet, which had been lost long ago. It was blue, too. Did Cassidy pick this ring due to some unconscious memory? Or was it simply blue?

She brought her hand up to her mouth, and her lips found the rings. Brandy loved her. This was obvious. As a friend? Very much. Beyond that.. the older ring on her finger wouldn't allow such thoughts.

It can't be. It's pointless.

"The asparagus is still a giant frozen block!" came Pete's voice from the kitchen as Sandy opened the door for Cassidy and Brandy.

"But the salmon is okay?" Cassidy asked in exaggerated pleading, grabbing the wine bottle fiercely, "that was the deal, see? I bring the wine, and there's salmon, and I –"

"Oh, shut your mouth and get in here, girls," Sandy chuckled, "Pete, throw on some mash or something."

The Lowe household was as tidy and conservatively decorated as one might expect from a middle aged couple. A thick wood table that looked like an heirloom, a sizable wall clock to match, a few plants here and there that might have been synthetic. A classy but understated light fixture hung over the dining room table, taking cues from olden grand chandeliers.

As soon as Cassidy and Brandy got seated, Pete plunked fairly full glasses of red wine in front of them both.

"Shame, ladies, you should know salmon pairs with red!"

Brandy held up the white whine they'd brought. "What about this?"

Pete shrugged. "We chug it after dinner. Or you chug it quickly before dinner's ready. The potatoes are going to be ten minutes or so, because they're instant. I mean I've been working on them for the last half hour."

"I'm driving," Brandy said.

"You can still drive with a fairly high blood/potato level," Pete assured her.

"We finally got ya over here," Sandy said as she came in from another room. "It's good to meet one of Cassidy's friends, and most of them are attached to base, so it's not all that easy, when their off time is already claimed by family and stuff."

"Plain ole' civilian me," Brandy said, taking a sip of the red wine.

Sandy hunkered in for motherly snooping/interrogation. "So, you've known Cassie for about forever, right? Before she joined the military?"

Old memories brought a soft smile to Brandy. "Yeah. By the time we became a couple though, she was already decided on it though, I just came along to make life complicated."

Sandy patted Brandy's hand a couple of times and chuckled. "Young love tends to do that."

Across the table, Cassidy was nursing her wine, looking gloomy. "I don't know how appropriate it is to talk about past romantic relationships ... sometimes." She put her hand on her chest to feel the ash-pendant below. It brought a sudden jarring silence to the room.

Brandy took an audible breath. "Sandy, I heard *you* have one of those."

Sandy took a moment to realize what Brandy was talking about, then nodded. She looked saddened by it. "Yes. Yes, I do. I originally was going to just get one, but with how things were… it seemed right for Cassie to have one too. I… I don't wear mine anymore."

Cassidy frowned slightly, and sat up straighter, as if offended.

"Oh, I have it of course, "Sandy continued, "tucked in a drawer upstairs. These days I only bring it out about once a year. Any more felt wrong."

"*You* don't have to punish yourself," Cassidy mumbled.

Sandy gasped. "Cassie! Neither do you! We've talked about this! Are you wearing it as… as *punishment*?"

Cassidy turned her head to side closing her eyes for a solid second and a half. "N..no… just remembrance."

Brandy got up, and moved behind Cassidy, putting her arms around Cassidy's shoulders. "No one expects you'll forget," Brandy said, "And *no one* wants you to feel punished."

This set Cassidy into tears, which set Brandy and Sandy off. Sandy made her away around and grabbed Brandy and Cassidy.

"See, and you caused a group hug, twit," Brandy chuckled between soft sobs.

Pete stood, sniffling. "Well… whew. I … those potatoes are probably almost– "

Sandy grabbed his arm, and yanked him into the hug. "Not so fast, tough guy." Pete joined in. "Well, she's right, Cassie. We've said it before, we don't blame you. You can't either. My roof, my rules. No blaming yourself."

"I'm not sure that's how it works, Pete." Cassidy said.

"Yup. I said so. Now seriously, the potatoes are going to be wrecked."

Dinner was served, and slow to leave the topic of the late Cheryl, stories were told of her happier times, and wine flowed freely.

"I told you all about the time she wanted to get a good look at one of those desert lizards?" Cassidy asked. Over the years, they'd all heard it, but it was a popular story, so no one stopped it. Ready to set out to find one, Cassidy stumbled upon one in the base, but ignored it, just to have an excuse to spend more time away from base with Cheryl.

Sandy and Pete's stories often had photos to go with them, such as her graduation, and first steps, but those got a little too sad, so they gently moved to other topics. National politics, indigenous relations, technology, it seemed every topic seemed to have a sub-section to avoid. A hidden road to Cheryl's death. But they avoided them.

At one point, Cassidy left the room to go to the washroom, but when she came back, Pete had wandered off, and Sandy was leaning over to Brandy, holding her hand on the table, and nodding.

"Hey, what's up?" Cassidy asked, feeling her ears burning.

"We decided you need a vacation," Brandy said.

"I'm *on* vacation *right now*," Cassidy said with a shrug. "What, you want to take me somewhere warm with lots of sand? Cuz that's a lot like my work."

"There's no ocean at your base," Sandy said dryly. "Go to an igloo-resort, just somewhere you only have to relax, and drink silly colourful drinks."

Cassidy sat and lifted her wine. "Well, one colour down."

They finished up dinner, chatted, and kept going with the wine. Brandy had stopped at one, for sake of driving. No one seemed overly eager to break into the white. Eventually, Brandy and Cassidy were heading out. Sandy noticed Cassidy adjust the strap of her ash-pendant.

"Did you put that on for tonight?" Sandy asked quietly.

Cassidy touched the pendant through her top. "No. I always have it on."

Sandy sighed, and brought Cassidy in for a hug. "Don't let it get too heavy. It wasn't meant to hurt you."

The trip back to Brandy's wasn't particularly chatty. Brandy tried to start some talk during the drive. "So... *they're* super nice."

"Yeah. Hey, how many glasses of wine did I have?" Cassidy mumbled.

"Feelin' it? I think it was at least three."

"*Three?* Isn't that like half a bottle?"

"It wasn't a small bottle, Cass, but one way or another, yeah, you had the lion's share."

"Rarr," Cassidy said as she slumped against the car interior. "Maybe she has a point, but respinsibdutyiy, blah blah, not what's she'd want. Heavy."

"You okay, Cass?"

"Quiet drunken Cassie time," Cassidy mumbled.

Brandy glanced over at Cassidy with a mix of amusement and pity, and drove on in silence.

Quiet drunken Cassie made it from car to house easily enough, perhaps a bit less drunken than before.

Brandy locked the door for the night, and headed to the washroom. "Be right back." When Brandy came out, she found that Cassidy hadn't gone far at all.

Cassidy stood in the living room, holding her necklace out at arms' length, with the ash-containing pendant dangling at the bottom.

And she stared at it. "I know it's morbid." She flung the cord around so that the pendant sat in her hand. "Did I ever tell you, I was with her," Cassidy inhaled sharply to fight crying. "– held her hand as she died?"

Brandy lowered her gaze. She *had* heard the tale before, but similar to the lizard story, the telling of it seemed important right now, so she remained silent.

Cassidy gripped the pendant tighter, closing her eyes just as tight. Her breathing became rougher. She yelled, and threw the pendant to the floor as hard as she could.

Brandy took half a step forward before Cassidy collapsed to her knees. Her hand rested on top of the pendant, she remembered Cheryl's hand in the last moments. Remembered her auburn hair spread on the floor around her head.

"*Bleeding out, barely able to look around.*" She looked at her hand, remembering Cheryl's blood. Cassidy made a sound birthed from a roar and a scream, and sunk into heaving sobs. "Minutes... Before... Just fine... if I'd been there..."

"You might have been killed too," Brandy said softly, kneeling down to put a hand on Cassidy's shoulder.

Cassidy threw Brandy's hand aside. "*And you think that would have bothered me?!*"

Brandy yelled right at Cassidy's face, "*It would have bothered others. It would have bothered me.*" Brandy threw her arm around Cassidy's sobbing frame, intent on just squeezing until the tremors eased.

"You think I haven't heard that speech before?" Cassidy grumbled.

"Is it any less true?"

Cassidy didn't reply for a while. The sobbing calmed, bit by bit. "It makes me a burden," she finally murmured out.

"Bullshit, hon, you mean it makes the people who love you a burden to you."

Cassidy sniffled. "The thought occurred to me once or –"

"Too bad, buttercup," Brandy said, "deal with it. We can burden each other."

Teetering between crying and a giggle, Cassidy thought of that therapist she hadn't seen in years. "Doesn't sound healthy."

"Whatever. Know what *is* healthy?" Brandy picked up the pendant. "This getting off your neck." She tucked it into Cassidy's pocket. "Remember. But don't be its slave."

For a time, they simply held each other.

"Thank you," Cassidy said softly, breaking the silence.

"What the hell for?"

"Putting up with me."

"Ha. Cass, I've been putting up with you for about a decade now."

"Yeah, and I keep making it harder."

Brandy chuckled slightly. "Yup. But I don't plan on going anywhere."

"You're crazy. A sane person would flee."

"Probably. It's late, you have a bunch of wine in ya. Go to bed."

Day 3

The morning came, close to eleven A.M., and Cassidy staggered into the kitchen, dressed for the day in a t-shirt and jeans. She found Brandy there, a tiny bit more dressy in a navy blouse and a simple above-the knee skirt.

"Mornin' Cass. I was about to make some toast, you want?"

"Sure, thanks." Cassidy put her hand down on the kitchen island, and a single ring made a tap. Just the blue cheap one that Brandy had bought her; no engagement ring. "Know what that means?"

Brandy started the toaster and looked over to Cassidy's hand. She sighed. "Does it mean Cassidy spent some time last night remembering Cassidy?"

Cassidy echoed Brandy's sigh. "I... yeah, I guess so." She turned the ring a bit on her finger. "I never used to be a jewellery person. Thank you, you saved me from being naked." She tapped the ring on the counter a couple of times with a smirk.

Brandy rolled her eyes, opening a cupboard. "Jam, PB, butter, marmalade, uh..."

"I can't say this means I'm 'fixed' though."

"Of course not, honey," Brandy said with a phony sweetness, "you're a lesbian, it would be redundant to get fixed."

Cassidy contained a snort. "You crazy bitch, I —" and she stopped herself.

A certain stillness seemed to drift through the room. Cassidy stared at her cheap yet meaningful ring, and Brandy stood, paused at the cupboard. Eventually, Cassidy dared to raise her eyes, and found herself staring at Brandy's back.

"Honey." Cassidy finally said. She could see Brandy take a quick, deep breath.

"Hm?"

"On my toast."

"Right," Brandy said, "I should have remembered."

"Honey never lasts on base. Gets eaten up so fast. I keep saying we should req more at a time, it's not like it goes bad, and it's warm enough there that it's not likely to —"

Ding.

The toaster saved them both from the ramblings of forced conversation. The preparation and consumption of toast gave them ample excuse not to talk. Moments when eyes met were awkward, and corrected quickly.

"This is stupid, are you okay, Cass?"

After a deep sigh, and catching an errant drip of honey on her thumb, Cassidy replied, "No, and yes. One thing starts to get simpler, and it opens a window to new issues."

"Vague, but okay. Anything that needs talking about?"

"Probably," Cassidy said, realizing how vague she remained.

"Zoo, movie, dinner?"

"Huh?"

"Suggestions for today."

"Zoo, huh?" Cassidy pondered while finishing her last bit of toast.

"Too cool for zoo, Cass?"

Cassidy did the gun-finger move. "You know it. But I can enjoy it... *ironically*. As long as there's cotton candy somewhere there."

"Ironic cotton candy, Ms. Hipster?"

"I prefer watermelon flavour. But you're groovin' my vibe."

"Always did."

The distraction of doing something a little on the childish side kept things light and breezy. At one point near the kangaroo enclosure, they spotted a very young couple, who were painfully, obviously in love.

"Who takes a date to the *zoo*?" Cassidy said under her breath.

"Maybe they're enjoying it ironically," Brandy answered in perfect deadpan.

Cotton candy, ironic or otherwise, was not to be found today.

Eventually, they found themselves parked in the lot of the theatre, in view of the movie listing, and monolithic posters to go with most of them. They were faced with the same issue of movie selection as at home.

"Dang," Cassidy said, sucking her teeth, "I was hoping they'd have 'Incident at Ganymede II: the Ganymedening'."

"Ganymede *Event*. I think. Number two got delayed because the director was caught with his pants down, late one night in the middle of a sheep pasture."

"Please tell me you're kidding."

"No, I'm pretty *sure* it was *Event* at Ganymede, not *Incident*."

"Dork. Okay, pick something, Brandy."

"How about the 3D kids' thing?"

"They're traps," Cassidy said, "tearjerkers in hiding."

"Not that studio. I'm sure this one is just insultingly crass humour."

"We need something intelligent, but not turning boring while trying to be intelligent."

"I'd take some stupidity to avoid being bored," Brandy said.

"Stupidity? Then let's call Nia!" Cassidy burst out laughing.

"You're awful!" Brandy said, trying to resist chuckling, "she's not particularly dumb!"

"Well, you're right. I barely know her. But you have to have know it'd be a waste of time. Trying to hook me up with her."

"Yeah, yeah. I've already said sorry," Brandy pouted.

"Was it some kind of test?" Cassidy asked, head askew.

"Test?"

"And what would you have done if Nia and I had hooked up?"

"I... would have been happy for you." Brandy gave her worst 'honest' face.

Cassidy raised an eyebrow. "Is that so?"

"No." Brandy paused for a moment, deep in thought. "She's too dumb for you."

They still needed to decide on a movie. Neither of them particularly wanted to see one, and as much as Cassidy felt like talking, she needed to digest what was happening in her head. A movie buys a little bit of time where she didn't have to force or evade conversation.

In the last twenty-four hours, she had taken off the ring, and the pendant that she clung to so vehemently. She felt guilty for taking them off, yet also a little freedom. Which led back to guilt.

"Spy flick," Brandy blurted, jostling Cassidy's train of thought. "Do we have any issues with a spy flick?"

"Deal, done, let's go."

In the movie, while Hero McHero uncovered international plots of biological weapons, Cassidy ran herself in mental circles. By reflex, she idled by fiddling with her ring, but of course her fingers found a different ring than had been the usual. It made her glance over to Brandy. She wasn't quite as young as when they had dated, but her wavy mane was as easy to gaze into as always. Her face hadn't so much as aged, as matured. Matured as in fully blossomed. She had dated a girl. This was a woman. *Stop staring, she'll notice.* Why was she staring? It was so easy to stare. Look away, look at your hands. The ring looked back at her. *Stop looking at your hands, you're in a movie, look at the damned movie.*

Her breathing had become heavier, and she felt on the edge of tears.

"*How did this get so fucked up?*" she whispered to herself.

Brandy heard, and turned to face her. "You okay?"

Cassidy swallowed hard, and nodded, facing the movie, and blinking back tears. Out of the corner of her eye, she saw Brandy's hand move to her own knee. Did that hand have a plan to move to Cassidy's hand? Or knee? Or was it waiting to be held?

"*Damned high-schooler thoughts,*" Cassidy scorned herself, "*don't over-think it. Could mean nothing. But…*"

She tried to watch the movie, but her mind wouldn't let her focus. She needed a walk. "I'm gonna dash to the washroom," she said before leaving at a brisk pace. Into the light, right to the washroom. She stood at the sink-counter and stared at her reflection.

"Don't cry," she thought, "What exactly am I crying over anyway? Giving up on Cheryl? Falling for Brandy? *Shit, am I falling for Brandy?* Am I rebounding? Longest damned rebound, five damned years."

She clenched her fist and felt her new ring. "Damn it!" She stomped her way back to her seat, and sat with her arms crossed, pissed off at herself. Enough that she managed to not be distracted by Brandy, no mater how magical she looked in the warmth of the dimmed lights, *damn it, stop it.*

"What's wrong?" Brandy whispered.

"Don't know. Do, but don't. No chatting in the movie, it's rude."

"You wanna ditch this movie?"

"Really?"

"Yeah, really. Dinner?"

"Sushi. Hanzo's."

"Good."

The trip to Hanzo's wasn't too talkative, but Cassidy had reeled back the self-loathing, now in a gentler mental fatigue. Describing Hanzo's as 'a sushi place', was a bit of a disservice. It was a fairly posh Japanese restaurant. A deep red facade interior hinting strongly to China, with traditional-style archways made for a warm, and decidedly dark welcome. The booth they ended up in felt almost like a private room, with decorative curtains draping over the edges a little.

"You can see where this is headed, as much as I can." Cassidy sighed, fumbling with her new ring.

"Yes." Brandy took a sip of saki. "You're going to try to fix me up with Nia."

Cassidy was forced into a smile, but quickly went into deadpan, quietly but forcefully replying in near monotone, "No, Nia is mine. I'll fight you for her, I'm a soldier with muscles and stuff, I'd win." She took the chance to browse the menu, and Brandy followed suit.

The saki was on the sweeter side. They both quietly went through the menus for a while, but Cassidy found that very little was making it to her brain.

She eventually slapped the open menu down onto the table front of herself.

"*How am I supposed to feel right now?*"

Brandy sat upright in surprise, near shock. "Feel? How…? What? How do *I* know? How *do* you feel?"

With a deflating sigh, Cassidy melted forward, hands and forehead against the table. "*Terrified!* Entirely, totally terrified!"

"…of?"

Cassidy sat up a bit, but not so far as to risk eye contact. "Of you! Of you rejecting me, of me neglecting you, of me betraying Cheryl's memory, which is crap I've all logically worked out, but I'm carrying all this crap, and I don't know what to do with it!"

Brandy stared at the deflated Cassidy for a moment, and finally gave her best suggestion. "Stuff it."

"Excuse me?"

"Stuff it. You know full well that it's all bullshit, so stuff it. Who's ring are you wearing, Cass?"

"Yours."

"No, that's *your* ring, to make you remember *you*."

"Now *that's* bullshit, Brandy. I'll never see this ring and *not* think of you."

Brandy sighed. "I'm sorry. That wasn't my intent."

"It will make me think of how much you care for some reason. How much you're there for me. How much you try to help for some reason."

"Why?" Brandy looked to her side as if someone might be there to show her a cue card. "Why do I care? Do I have to say it?"

"Brandy…"

"It's been over a decade I've known you, Cass. There has not been a time… not when you were with Cheryl, not even when I broke up with you and blocked your calls… there has not been a time when I haven't loved you in *some* capacity or another. I know you'll always be a part of my life. I want to help you because it hurts to see you hurting, because I love you. As a friend, always. Above that? I..."

"I don't deserve you," Cassidy mumbled.

"*Well, you're damned right you don't!* We know you ended up as a crappy girlfriend, and no one needs that hurt again! And you've been moping for five years, and I've done what I can to drag you through that! That's a lot of work, you know?!"

Cassidy could only nod in shame.

"But..." Brandy said, "you've grown. I ... I can't imagine you ever taking me for granted again. That's been burnt out of you the hard way."

Head still low, a tear dropping into the table, with a shaky voice, Cassidy begged, "Do... Do I have the right – have I earned the right to say it?"

"Earned?" Brandy put her hand on Cassidy's. "I don't know. But you *have* the right to say whatever you want, either way." Brandy's breathing betrayed nervous expectation.

Cassidy swallowed hard, and clenched Brandy's hand, but still couldn't bear eye contact. "I... I love you."

"'Bout time you figured that out."

Cassidy looked up to see Brandy crawling over the table to grab her face, and stare her in the eye. Brandy's hair flowed down around both their faces, and they stared. Complications crawled back into their little dark spaces, and what darkness remained embraced them both.

Brandy lowered her face a bit more until their foreheads met, eyes closed. They had touched many times during this trip, but now, they truly *touched*. It was new, thrilling and terrifying somehow. Like a first touch.

"You're pretty brave," Cassidy sighed.

"You mean *insane*."

Cassidy crawled forward, teasing Brandy's lips with her own as she joined her on the table.

Brandy wrapped her arms around Cassidy, and chuckled softly, "this room isn't –" but she was silenced when Cassidy's lips grazed hers. Soft and timid, wanting to preserve their 'first' kiss. Brandy closed her eyes, lips still parted, and just felt Cassidy's lips slide softly against her own. She then felt Cassidy's hand on her hip, sliding up under the edge of her top.

"Cassie... Cassie.. we're on a table in a restaurant."

"Really? Thanks for keeping me abreast of the situation." Cassidy changed to a deeper, more aggressive kiss, and her hand followed similar intents.

Letting the kiss, and the touch take her mind, Brandy eventually had to break for air, when she whispered, "we're going to get arrested."

"I'll arrest them right back." Cassidy seriously considered stripping Brandy down right on the table.

"You haven't been an M.P. for years." Brandy slid off the table onto Cassidy's side, miraculously not knocking over any Saki, and at no point quite stopping kissing Cassidy. Cassidy followed. "How about under the table?"

"Probably too much used gum."

Whether the waitress was waiting to see if Cassidy and Brandy planned on getting off the table, or her timing was just really good, she showed up, notepad in hand "And have we decided what we want?"

"I think we finally did," Cassidy chirped up, beaming.

"Yeah, what do we owe ya for the Saki?"

With a small bill overpaid for the sake of haste, they rushed to the car and were underway. Enthusiasm got Cassidy's hand on Brandy's knee quickly, but self control and wanting Brandy to drive efficiently home for the chance to really let loose, kept her hand from going further. She watched Brandy's breathing deepen from the touch, and found her own breathing getting harder, the longer she stared at the breathing motions of Brandy's chest.

Brandy glanced quickly to Cassidy, and chuckled softly to see where Cassidy was looking. In response, she freed a hand from driving to open up a couple of buttons. Cassidy leaned over to cuddle up, putting her head on Brandy's shoulder, partly to get a better view down her top.

"Oh, pesky bra," Cassidy whispered. A momentary urge pushed Cassidy's hand up Brandy's lap, pushing her skirt up a bit with it.

"Driving here," Brandy softly joked. "You don't want to wrap around a tree now."

Cassidy slid her hand up to liberate a third button on Brandy's top. "I don't think there's any laws against driving topless."

"Behave. We'll be home in like two minutes. I can see the driveway."

Cassidy ran her hand below Brandy's bust-line, and with a careful lift, she gently raised Brandy's cleavage, and watched the plumping display down her top. It was magnificent with Brandy's intensified breathing, and a soft gasp.

"I'm gotta take something off," Cassidy growled. She plucked open one more button quickly, before reaching behind her own head, and yanking out her hairband, releasing her ponytail into a mane fit for a hunter. Feeling the car park, she planned to lunge face first into Brandy's bra, but she was thwarted by Brandy's own lunge, a deep, hungry kiss, as her hands ran through Cassidy's hair.

"*I* wanted to take that thing off of you, Cassie." Brandy opened the door on Cassidy's side, and slowly crawled over Cassidy to get out. Legs straddling over Cassidy for a moment, Brandy shifted her hips to ensure that her skirt rode up enough to give Cassidy a peek at her panties, and pausing for a sweet little grind as she did her best to press her chest against Cassidy's face before moving off, and out of the car. Cassidy's efforts to partake were short-lived. Brandy was off, and giggling towards her front door.

She was fast enough to outpace Cassidy's fumbling, and was quickly inside, with the door open, awaiting Cassidy.

Cassidy pounced in pursuit, pausing just inside the door, in a pose ready to strike. Her seldom-free hair was tossed with the sudden stopping, landing across her shoulder.

Brandy stood ahead, wide eyed. In awe. In shock. She held one hand on her chest, and other other outstretch to stop Cassidy.

"Brandy?"

Brandy, smiling wide, began silently crying, and her hand held out, now pointed at Cassidy. "Th… there she is."

Cassidy looked around to double check that no one followed her in the door, and no, Brandy was staring right at Cassidy.

"There she is," Brandy's voice broke, and the crying pushed itself more. "there she is, there's … there's my Cassie. I … wasn't sure if I'd find her, but there she is."

Cassidy stood tall, and thumbed her new ring, staring at the woman who never gave up on her. Her love.

Brandy just stared back at Cassidy and smiled. "There's my Cassie, she's alive. I remember her."

Watching Yute

Cassidy's original story, this full length novel tells of her time with Cheryl, and the surrounding trials of sorrow, justice and revenge.

As part of the Lifehack series, Watching Yute is a science-fiction tale, which deals with the abuses of nanotechnology, the resulting conflicts, and the impact on the people caught in the middle.

While Watching Yute is the least action-laden of the series, Cassidy's troubled road makes is easily the most dramatic and personal.

RUBBERMAN'S
CAGE

Lenth grew up in a lie.

Apparently there's more than five people in the world.

Four Brothers live their lives in an enclosed habitat as directed by the silent Rubberman above them. When they disobey, they get shocked. This is normal. It always has been.

When a Brother dies, they learn of death. When he is replaced by someone new, they learn they are replaceable.

When the ceiling above the ceiling cracks open, Lenth plans a journey beyond the known universe:

A third floor.
Up.

Coming soon, the second book in the Rubberman series:

RUBBERMAN'S
CITIZENS

In Citizenry, Leena knew cruelty was normal.

Order was kept by Warren, through intimidation and abuse.
Normal meant hearing screams, and knowing no one dared help.

Normal was knowing that tomorrow,
it could be your own screams being ignored.

Leena found a way to help. Leena found a chance.
Leena discovered revolution.

Also check out the rest of the Lifehack series:

Starting with *Lifehack*, continuing in *Watching Yute,* and concluding in *Echoes of Erebus*. Love, loss, nanotech-driven evils, and a madman who refuses to accept death as the end.

LIFEHACK

Regan has her ups and downs.
- Dumping her girlfriend: Down.
- Moving in with her loving brother: Up.
- Waking up to a plague of undead: REALLY down.

After the undead began roaming the neighborhood, Regan lost track of her brother. She's spent the last two years searching for him. In the meantime, she's fallen in love, only to be told, "Sorry, I'm straight. And you're a lunatic." There's a psycho out there somewhere who caused the outbreak, using nanotechnology, just for the fun of it, and Regan intends to hunt him down.

Oh, and the crush she still has on the straight gal? Dangerously distracting, when there's a zombie around every corner.

WATCHING YUTE

An ideal post opened up for Lieutenant Cassidy Stanton when she wanted a fresh start. She expected a measure of peace, guarding a historic temple in the middle of the desert.
She didn't expect to find a new girlfriend; maybe even a soul mate.
She didn't expect to be in the crossfire of a terrorist, a cowardly scientist, and a fleet of microscopic invaders.
She didn't expect to lose.

ECHOES OF EREBUS

Sarah's got daddy issues. He lives in her head, built her out of fish, and killed millions of people.
But he's really sorry.
Honest.

A father that lives in your head wouldn't be so bad if he wasn't the killer of millions. At least it's comforting to know that he didn't murder the fishes used to create your body.
Or the seagull.

Sarah hides her illegal nanite origins in an effort to build an orLeenary life, but the legacy of dad's horrors makes it difficult. Especially when new but familiar zombie-like abominations begin to appear in the city.

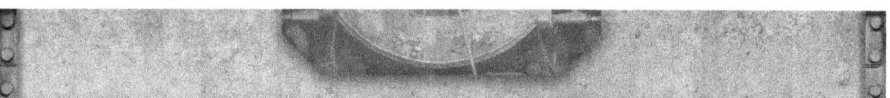

Find info on Joseph Picard's books at:

OZERO.CA

And Amazon.com.

www.ingramcontent.com/pod-product-compliance
Lightning Source LLC
Chambersburg PA
CBHW071355130626
46556CB00005B/2197

* 9 7 8 0 9 8 1 3 9 6 0 3 3 *